For Sophie

KESTREL BOOKS
Published by Penguin Books Ltd
Harmondsworth, Middlesex, England

Copyright © 1982 by Jan Ormerod

First published in 1982

ISBN 0 7226 5749 8
Printed and bound in Great Britain by
William Clowes (Beccles) Limited, Beccles and London

Jan Ormerod

Moonlight

Kestrel Books

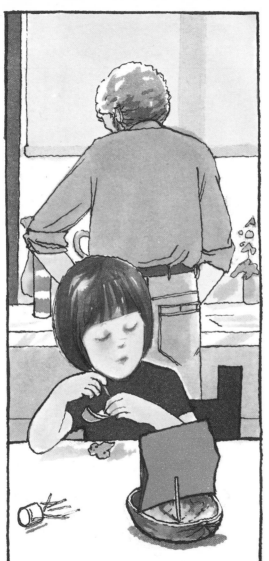

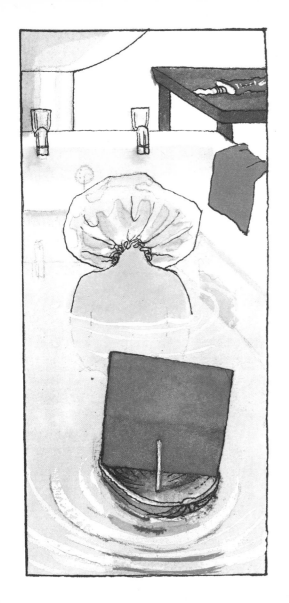

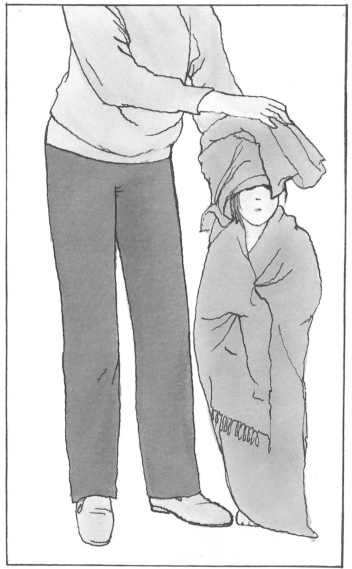

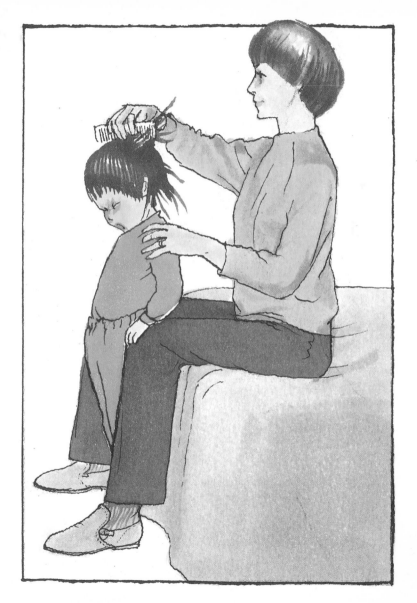

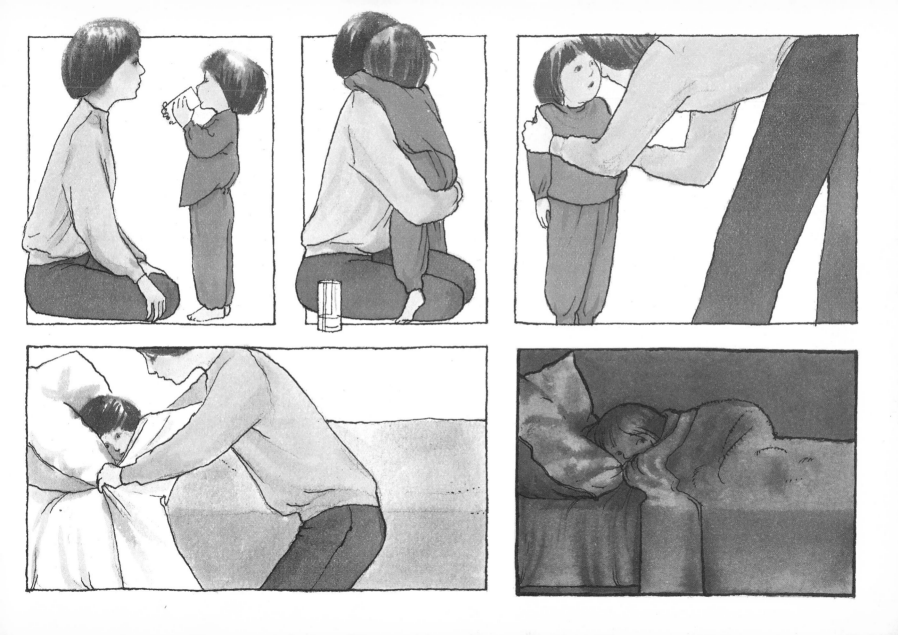

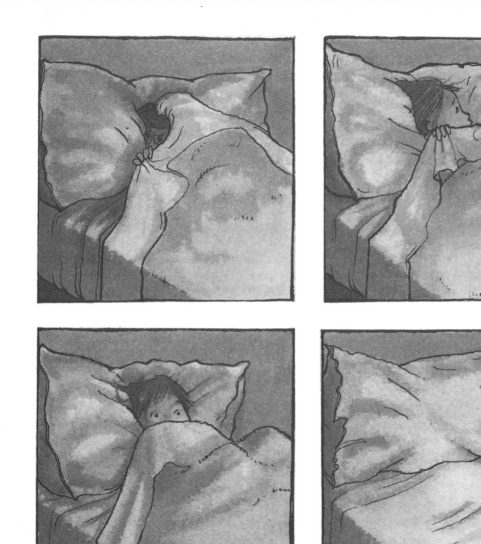

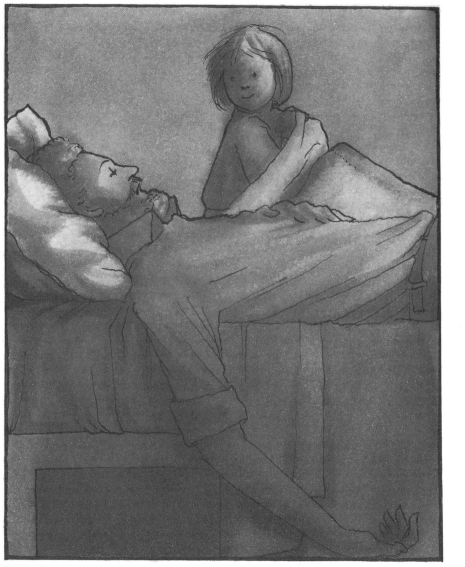

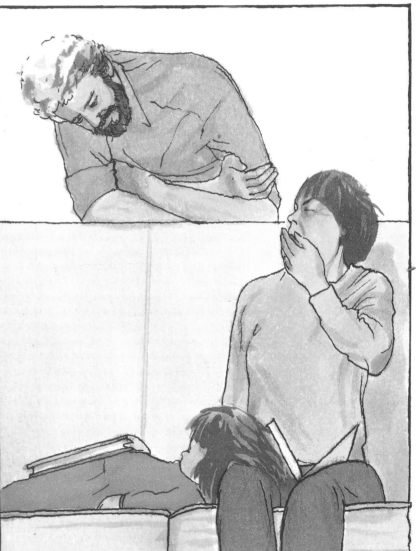

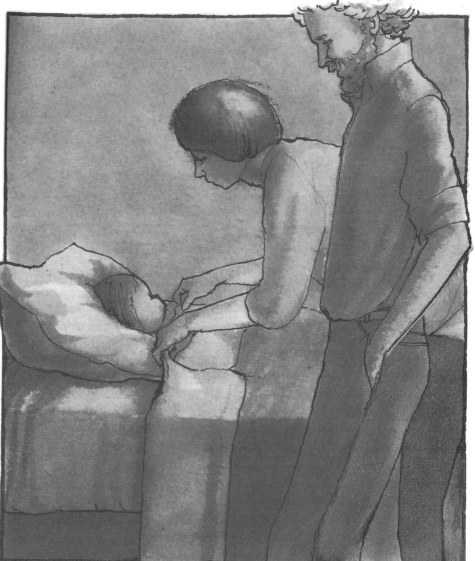